NOAH AND THE ZIZ

JACQUELINE JULES

ILLUSTRATED BY
KATHERINE JANUS KAHN

KAR-BEN
PUBLISHING

To Barbara, for giving me the idea, and to Kathy,
whose pictures inspired me.
—JJ

To David, for his loving and
consistent support of my work.
—KJK

Text copyright © 2005 by Jacqueline Jules
Illustrations copyright © 2005 by Katherine Janus Kahn

Kar-Ben Publishing, Inc.
A division of Lerner Publishing Group
241 First Avenue North
Minneapolis, MN 55401 U.S.A.
1-800-4KARBEN

Website address: www.karben.com

Library of Congress Cataloging-in-Publication Data

Jules, Jacqueline, 1956–
    Noah and the Ziz / by Jacqueline Jules ; illustrations by Katherine Janus Kahn.
        p.   cm.
    Summary: The Ziz, a huge and clumsy but well-meaning bird, tries to help
Noah gather all the animals together before the flood, but his strength,
size, and enthusiasm create some problems.
        ISBN: 0–929371–01–1 (lib. bdg. : alk. paper)
        ISBN: 1-58013-121-2 (pbk. : alk. paper)
        [1. Animals, Mythical—Fiction. 2. Noah (Biblical figure)—Fiction. 3. Animals—Fiction.]
    I. Kahn, Katherine, ill. II. Title.
    PZ7.J92927No 2004
    [E]—dc22   2003026442

Manufactured in the United States of America
1 2 3 4 5 6 – JR – 10 09 08 07 06 05

NOAH

had only one week to load the ark before the great flood. That was not much time to get ready.

"My hands are full," Noah told God. "I need to gather leaves for the giraffes and load hay for the cows. How can I go off in one direction to get the pandas and another direction to get the kangaroos? Please, God, I need help."

God listened to Noah's request. And God called the Ziz.

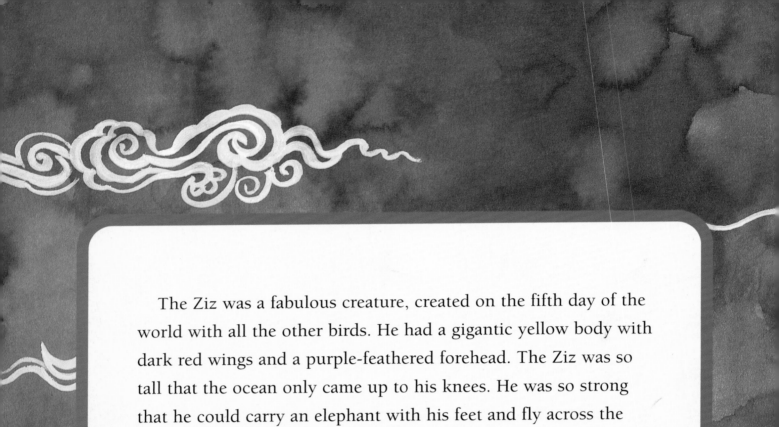

The Ziz was a fabulous creature, created on the fifth day of the world with all the other birds. He had a gigantic yellow body with dark red wings and a purple-feathered forehead. The Ziz was so tall that the ocean only came up to his knees. He was so strong that he could carry an elephant with his feet and fly across the world in twenty minutes. And the Ziz loved important jobs.

When God called him to Mount Sinai, the Ziz danced on the mountain top, flapping his wings.

"Collecting animals! That's a great job! When do I start?"

"Right away," God said.

The Ziz spread his huge wings and flew straight to the ark.

He circled until he saw a man with white hair carrying a load of hay on his back. The Ziz plopped down.

"Here I am!"

Noah was so surprised by the giant bird who had tumbled from the sky that he dropped his pile of hay.

"Who are you?" Noah asked.

"I'm Ziz! God sent me to collect the animals for you." The Ziz flapped his wings. They made such a wind that it blew the hay all around.

"I've been waiting for help," said Noah. "We don't have much time before the flood."

"That's right," Ziz answered. "I'll get started."

Noah bent down to pick up the hay.

The Ziz did not stay and help.

He stretched his huge wings and flew off to a watery swamp.

A few minutes later, he dropped down right in front of two alligators taking a nap. Plop!

Mr. and Mrs. Alligator opened their eyes and stared at the giant yellow bird splashing in the swamp.

"Today's your lucky day!" Ziz shouted.

The alligators did not have time to ask questions. Before they knew it, the Ziz lifted them by their tails. With Mrs. Alligator in his right foot and Mr. Alligator in his left foot, the Ziz flew back to the ark, singing:

**Flap! Flap! I'm as fast as fast can be!
Saving lives is the job for me!**

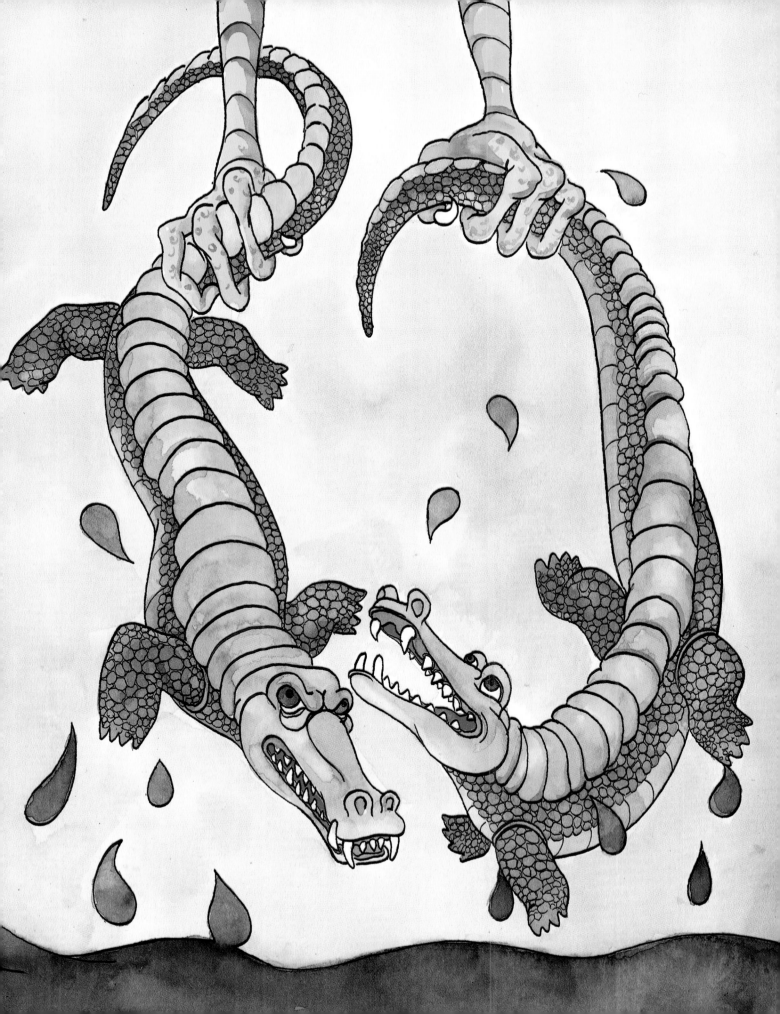

The Ziz dropped Mr. and Mrs. Alligator right in front of Noah. Plop! "Here they are!" Ziz sang. "The first two animals!"

Noah put down a load of leaves to look. "How long did they hang by their tails?" he asked. "Are they all right?"

"Just fine!" Ziz flapped his wings proudly, making such a wind that it blew the leaves all around.

"*Be careful,*" Noah said, bending down to pick up the mess.

The Ziz did not stay to help gather the leaves.

The Ziz flew off to a grassy plain where two zebras were grazing, and plopped down.

"Today's your lucky day! I'm going to save you!"

Mr. and Mrs. Zebra backed away from the giant yellow bird dancing in the grass.

"From what?" Mr. Zebra asked.

The Ziz didn't take the time to explain. He grabbed Mr. and Mrs. Zebra with his right foot. Then he saw Mr. and Mrs. Tiger. He grabbed them with his left foot and flew back to the ark, singing:

Flap! Flap! I'm as fast as fast can be!
Saving lives is the job for me!

This time, the Ziz didn't make the mistake of carrying them by their tails. He carried them by their stripes until he reached the ark and dropped them at Noah's feet. Plop!

"Be careful!" Noah said. "It hurts to be dropped."

The Ziz shook his purple-feathered head. He hated that word *careful*. Why was Noah always saying it?

The Ziz went back to work. He picked up elephants, kangaroos, horses, lions, pandas, reindeer, monkeys, gorillas, and giraffes—two of every large animal on earth. At the end of the day, the Ziz found Noah walking onto the ark with a load of bananas.

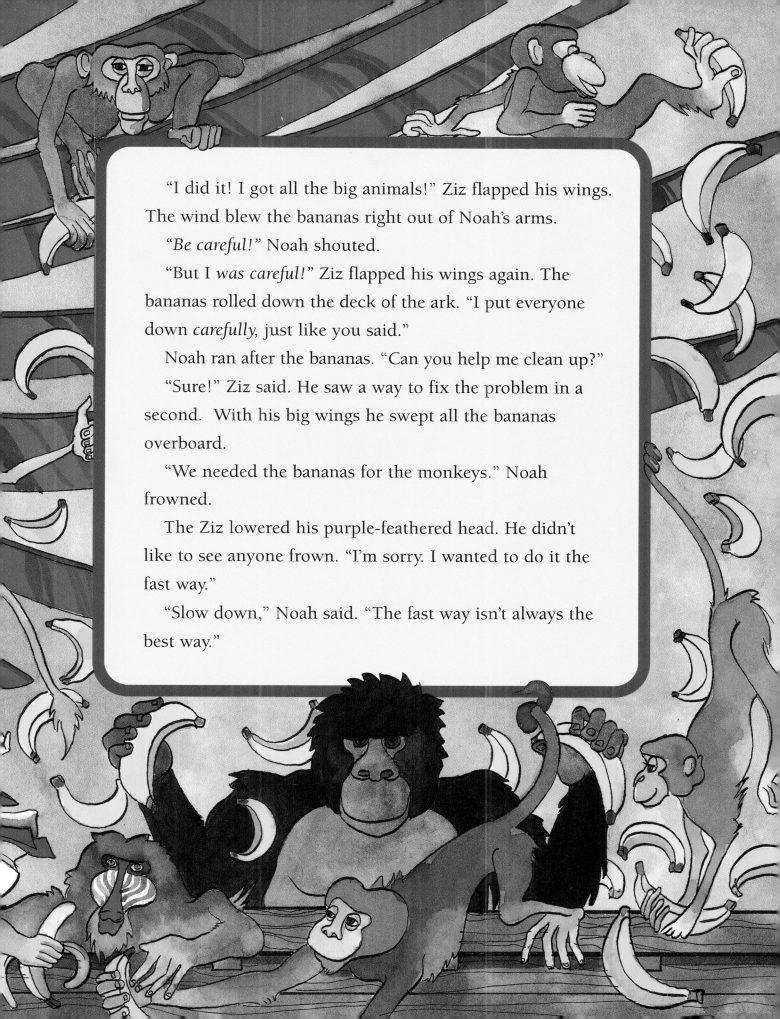

"I did it! I got all the big animals!" Ziz flapped his wings. The wind blew the bananas right out of Noah's arms.

"*Be careful!*" Noah shouted.

"But I *was careful!*" Ziz flapped his wings again. The bananas rolled down the deck of the ark. "I put everyone down *carefully,* just like you said."

Noah ran after the bananas. "Can you help me clean up?"

"Sure!" Ziz said. He saw a way to fix the problem in a second. With his big wings he swept all the bananas overboard.

"We needed the bananas for the monkeys." Noah frowned.

The Ziz lowered his purple-feathered head. He didn't like to see anyone frown. "I'm sorry. I wanted to do it the fast way."

"Slow down," Noah said. "The fast way isn't always the best way."

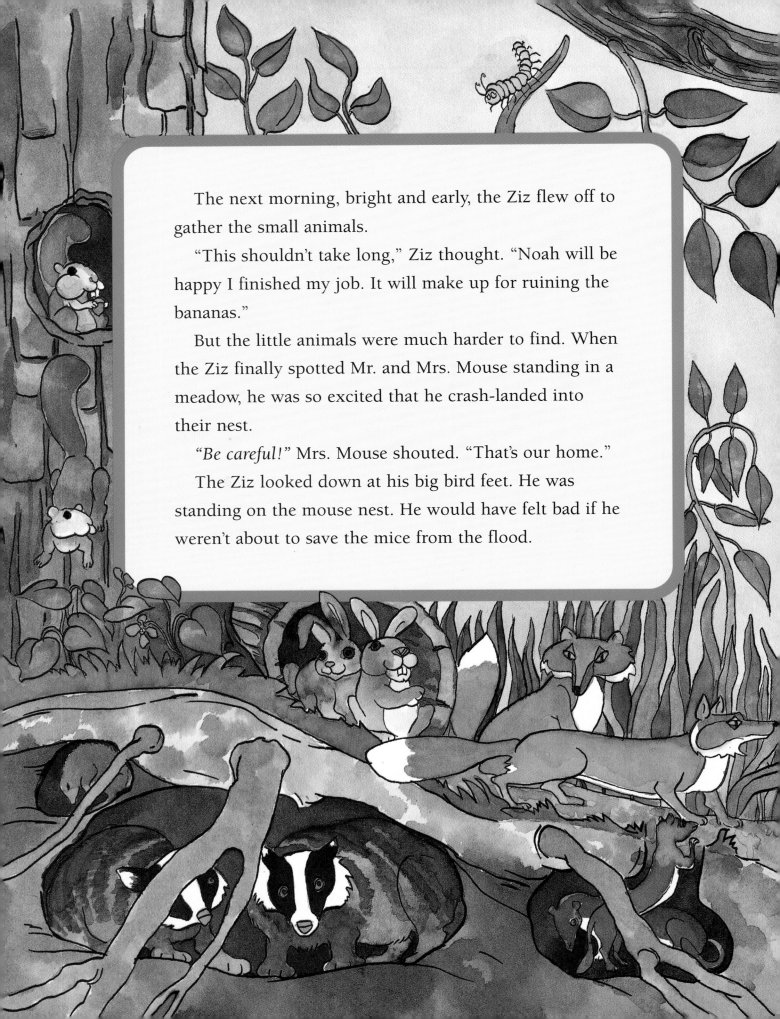

The next morning, bright and early, the Ziz flew off to gather the small animals.

"This shouldn't take long," Ziz thought. "Noah will be happy I finished my job. It will make up for ruining the bananas."

But the little animals were much harder to find. When the Ziz finally spotted Mr. and Mrs. Mouse standing in a meadow, he was so excited that he crash-landed into their nest.

"*Be careful!*" Mrs. Mouse shouted. "That's our home."

The Ziz looked down at his big bird feet. He was standing on the mouse nest. He would have felt bad if he weren't about to save the mice from the flood.

"You don't need your nest. I'm here to take you to the ark."
Ziz flapped his wings. The wind made the two little mice roll
like balls down a hill.

"Come back! Come back!" Ziz shouted, running after them.
The mice scurried away and hid in a small hole at the bottom
of a tree. The Ziz put his big eye against the hole.
"Come out," he cried.
"No!" the mice said. "We don't want to go with you!"

"What will I do now?" The Ziz sat down to think. He covered his purple-feathered head with his red wings, hoping to come up with a plan. No ideas came.

Finally, he decided to do what he always did when he was in trouble. He flew off to Mount Sinai to talk to God.

"The mice won't come with me," Ziz complained.

"Did you talk to Noah about this?" God asked.

"I don't want to talk to Noah." Ziz slumped over and pouted. "He's always telling me to slow down and *be careful*."

"I see," said God quietly. There was silence for a few moments.

"What should I do?" Ziz asked.

"Listen to Noah," God said.

"But the flood is coming," Ziz said. "There's no time to slow down." Ziz flapped his wings.

"Try it," God said firmly.

The Ziz flew away from Mount Sinai with his head hanging low. It wasn't easy to try a new way of doing things. But he wanted God and Noah to be proud of him.

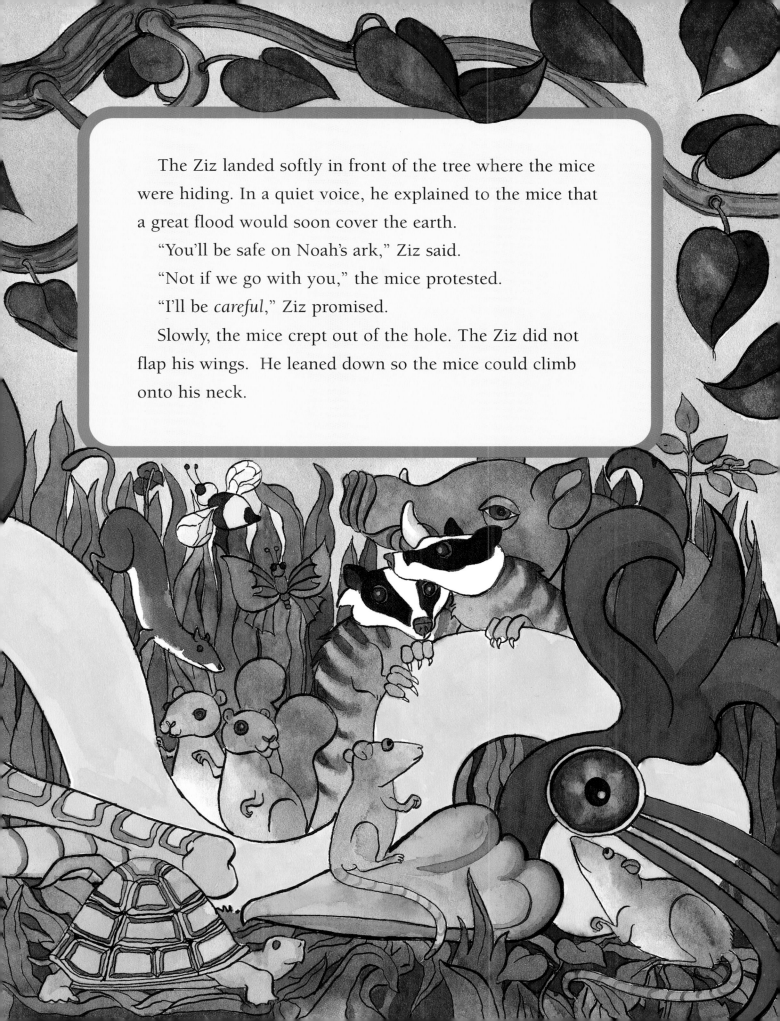

The Ziz landed softly in front of the tree where the mice were hiding. In a quiet voice, he explained to the mice that a great flood would soon cover the earth.

"You'll be safe on Noah's ark," Ziz said.

"Not if we go with you," the mice protested.

"I'll be *careful*," Ziz promised.

Slowly, the mice crept out of the hole. The Ziz did not flap his wings. He leaned down so the mice could climb onto his neck.

At the end of the day, the Ziz flew back to Noah with Mr. and Mrs. Mouse, Mr. and Mrs. Caterpillar, Mr. and Mrs. Bunny, and lots of other little animals riding on his broad yellow back. When he arrived at the ark, he stretched out his right wing, so the little animals could walk down easily.

"Good job!" Noah said, just as the first raindrops fell.
The Ziz nodded his purple-feathered head and smiled.

Flap! Flap! I'm as fast as fast can be!
Saving lives is the job for me!